Published by English Heritage
23 Savile Row
London W1S 2ET

Copyright © authors, illustrator and English Heritage 2003

First published by English Heritage 2003

Edited by Val Horsler
Designed by Brian Shields, Design Systems
Printed in England by Printco

ISBN 1 85074 829 2

C50, 5/03, PC 50681

Robbers at the Abbey
A Cuthbert story

Nicky and Humphrey Welfare
Illustrations by Sue Shields

'That's the one!
He's smiling!'

Granny often took Anna and Ben for trips in the holidays in her little car.
Today they had been to the old Abbey.
Granny tried to tell them what happened when the monks lived there long ago.

In the shop Granny said that they could buy one special treat.
At last they chose the bear, whose name was Cuthbert.
He seemed to be laughing and winking at them.

On the way home to Granny's cottage they took it in turns to talk to Cuthbert. Cuthbert said nothing.

Later, when they were tucked up in bed, they each held one of Cuthbert's paws.

'What do you think it was really like in the Abbey when the monks lived there, before the buildings fell down …?' wondered Anna.

Then Cuthbert winked. 'I can show you,' he said.

'Hold my paws tight.'

Suddenly they were back at the Abbey, but it was not a ruin any more. Cuthbert showed them how some of the monks were farmers, and how the others wrote beautiful books,

prayed in the church, or looked after people who were ill.

He took them into the Abbey.
They peeped through a door and could see the monks singing in the candlelight.

Just then Ben saw three figures at the far end of the church.
One was very fat, one was very thin, and one was very tall.
'Cuthbert, who are they?' he asked.

'They don't belong here,' said Cuthbert, looking worried.
'Let's follow them.'
The children tiptoed out of the church and into the garden.

Fat, Thin and Tall were nowhere to be seen.
'Where did they go?' whispered Anna.
Cuthbert was thinking. 'I know; they've gone to look for the Treasury.'
'The Treasury? What's that?' exclaimed Anna and Ben together.
'It's a special room where the monks and the rich people keep some of their most precious things,' explained Cuthbert.
'Those three must be trying to steal them'.

Cuthbert led Anna and Ben to the door of the Treasury.
Inside, Fat, Thin and Tall were stuffing their sacks with gold and silver.
Just then the Abbey bells began to ring. The monks were starting to come out of the church.
Fat, Thin and Tall were frightened. They had to escape.

The door of the Treasury was very tiny. Thin darted through first, carrying the sack.

Fat came out next. He only just managed to squeeze through sideways. Finally there was Tall who was feeling left behind.
He tried to run through after them and – WALLOP – he cracked his head on the stone above the door and – THUMP – he hit the ground.

'Quick! Lock the door! Now after them!' cried Cuthbert, pointing to Fat and Thin. Fat and Thin ran back into the garden. Anna, Ben and Cuthbert followed as fast as they could but when they got there...

... Fat and Thin had disappeared again. Only one door was open. Some delicious smells were coming from inside.

Anna pushed the door open. It was the dining room and all the tables were piled high with food, ready for a special holiday meal for the monks. There was Fat! He had stopped to taste all the dishes; they were so good and he was so greedy, that he had forgotten that he was running away from anyone.

'We'll lock this one in here.' said Cuthbert. 'Look, that must be the key, hanging on that hook.'

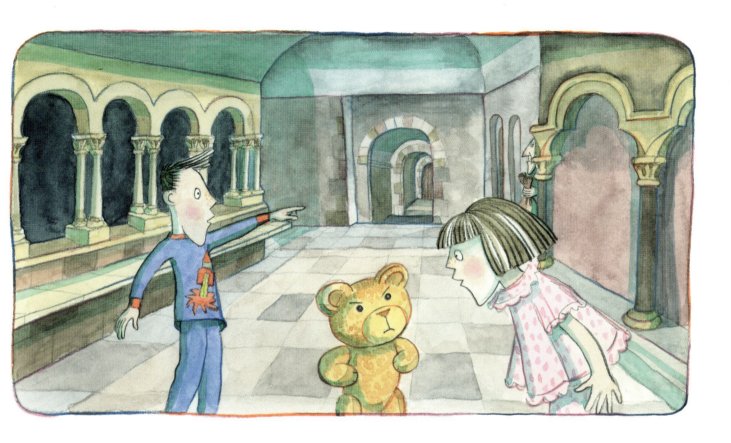

They tiptoed past Fat, unhooked the key and wriggled back under the tables.

Anna gently closed the door and Ben locked it.

'Well done,' said Cuthbert. 'Those two won't get up to any more mischief.'

'What do we do now?' whispered Anna.

'We have to find that third robber,' said Cuthbert.

'There he is!' cried Ben. He had just caught sight of Thin, hiding round a corner, a bulging bag in his hands.

Thin darted through a doorway and into a room...

...where a monk was sitting at his desk.
'Stop him! Stop thief!' shouted Anna and Ben. Thin tried to rush past the monk. CRASH! Thin knocked over the desk. There was black and red ink everywhere. The monk was furious and chased him out of the room, screeching 'Stop! You scruffy, ink-spilling monster!'

Thin ran outside and was chased round the buildings by Anna, Ben and Cuthbert.
Thin dived through a door into a workshop.

'Oh Cuthbert,' exclaimed Anna, 'the smell in the dining room was lovely but this is REVOLTING.' 'Er ... well.' whispered Cuthbert. 'The smell is coming from those big tanks. This is the tannery where the monks make leather by soaking sheep skins in chicken poo and horse wee. It's disgusting! Quick! Over there!'

Thin thought that he had a chance to escape and ran towards the door. Cuthbert leaned across and pushed over a broom.

Thin, hurtling past in the gloom, tripped over the broom.
BAM – SPLOSH! He went head over heels into a tank full of stinking water. The bag flew out of his hand and landed on a pile of leather. Coins and silver plates tumbled out onto the ground.

'Poo! He stinks!' cried Anna. 'It's lucky he dropped the bag of treasure before he fell into the tank,' whispered a relieved Ben. 'I wouldn't want to have to fish it out of there. Yuk!'

Anna and Ben held their noses, and so did Cuthbert, as well as he could.

Other monks arrived, holding a dazed Tall and a very full, queasy Fat by the scruff of their necks.

They all roared with laughter when they saw smelly Thin. The monks were very, very pleased to get their precious things back safely. 'Cuthbert, you're a hero!' whispered Anna and Ben. 'This has been a very exciting trip,' chuckled Cuthbert, 'almost too exciting, but now it's time for us to go. Hold my paws tight.'

Suddenly, they were back in Granny's house.

The next day, Anna and Ben heard Granny talking on the phone. 'Oh yes, they enjoyed their day at the Abbey. They seem to know more about it than I do!'

Cuthbert just smiled.

You can see for yourself the abbey church in which Anna, Ben and Cuthbert spotted the robbers, the Treasury with its tiny door, and the tanks in the tannery that made Tall so smelly.

They are all at the beautiful Cistercian abbey at Rievaulx, 2 miles west of Helmsley, in North Yorkshire. The site is in the care of English Heritage and is open every day of the year, except for three days over Christmas and on New Year's Day.

PHOTOGRAPH: PAUL HIGHNAM
© ENGLISH HERITAGE

For more information about English Heritage,
or to become a member, please contact:

English Heritage Customer Services Department,
PO Box 569, Swindon SN2 2YP
telephone: 0870 333 1181; fax 01793 414926
e-mail: customers@english-heritage.org.uk

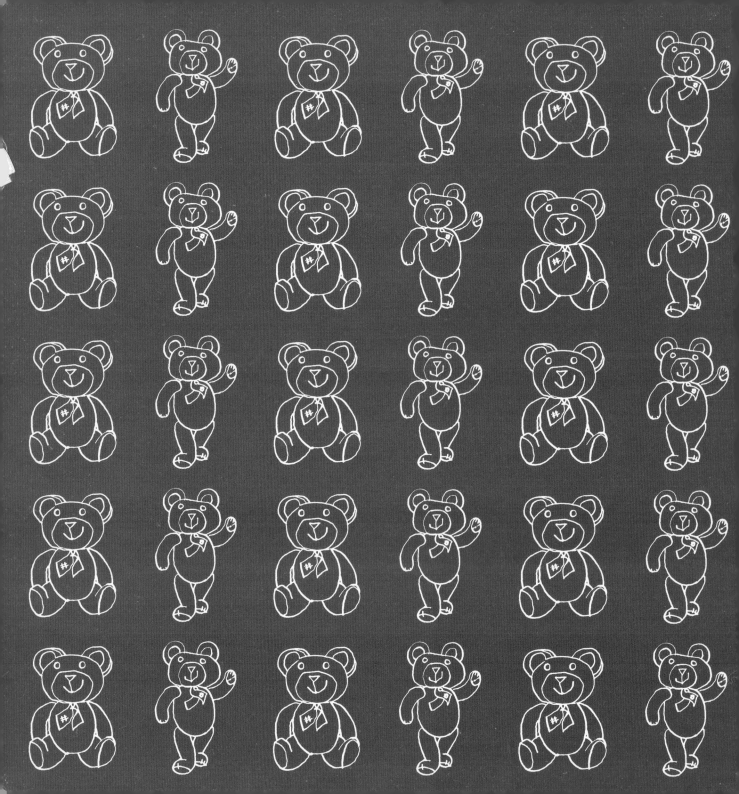